MR MONKEY

AND THE FAIRY TEA PARTY

MR MONKEY

AND THE FAIRY TEA PARTY

Linda Chapman

Illustrated by Sam Hearn

Orion
Children's Books

First published in Great Britain in 2015
by Orion Children's Books
an imprint of Hachette Children's Group
and published by Hodder and Stoughton Ltd
Orion House
5 Upper St Martin's Lane
London WC2H 9EA
An Hachette UK Company

1 3 5 7 9 10 8 6 4 2

The paper and board used in this paperback are natural and
recyclable products made from wood grown in sustainable forests.
The manufacturing processes conform to the environmental
regulations of the country of origin.

ISBN 978 1 4440 1552 2

A catalogue record for this book
is available from the British Library.

Printed and bound in China

www.orionchildrensbooks.co.uk

To Alexander Hopkinson who is very good at believing in magic – Mr Monkey would love to be your friend! L.C.

Contents

Chapter One

This is Mr Monkey.

He looks like any other cuddly
toy. But Mr Monkey is magic –
yes, magic!

Mr Monkey belongs to Class Two. His magic is secret, but one thing's for sure, exciting things always happen when the children take him home!

Miss Preston was choosing who was going to look after Mr Monkey for the week.

"Remember, whoever takes Mr Monkey home must write a diary about the things you do together," she told Class Two.

Rosie sat up as straight as she could. She hadn't looked after Mr Monkey but she really wanted to.

"Rosie. Why don't you take Mr Monkey this week?" said Miss Preston.

"Oh, Mr Monkey," Rosie whispered. "We're going to have so much fun."

Mr Monkey grinned. He liked the look of Rosie and he was sure they were going to have a **monkey-tastic** time!

Chapter Two

Rosie skipped out of school with Mr Monkey in her arms. Her mum was talking to Katie, Rosie's cousin.

Katie was a year older than Rosie. They had always been really good friends. They both loved fairies and always played fairy games together. But now Katie had gone into Class Three, things had changed. Katie said she didn't believe in magic and fairies were babyish.

Her mum spotted her.
"Hi, sweetie. Who's this?
He's very cute."

Rosie explained about
Mr Monkey.

Rosie's mum smiled. "We'll have to make sure he has an interesting week." She turned to Katie. "Why don't you come round tomorrow after school, Katie? You could bring your fairy dolls round."

"I don't play with fairies any more, Auntie Sally," said Katie. "I don't believe in magic." She glanced at a group of her Year Three friends who were standing nearby. "No one believes in magic in Class Three."

"Well, come for tea anyway," said Rosie's mum.

When Rosie got home she took Mr Monkey to the bottom of the garden. Hiding between the roots of an old oak tree were the fairy houses that Rosie and Katie had built. They were a bit dusty now. Rosie felt her tummy screw up as she imagined Katie seeing them and teasing her.

Rosie sat down and pulled her knees to her chest. She wished Katie would change back. She really missed her.

BOP!

Something small and hard hit Rosie on the head and bounced to the ground. It was an acorn.

BOP!

Rosie looked up.

Mr Monkey was sitting on the tree branch above her. "Hello, Rosie!" he called.

Chapter Three

Rosie squealed. "You're… you're alive!"

"It's lucky for you that I am because I can see you have a problem. Your silly cousin thinks she's too old for magic. We'll soon solve that!" said Mr Monkey.

"How?" asked Rosie.

"With a Mr Monkey Masterplan, of course! But first I need jam!" Mr Monkey said.

"Jam?" said Rosie.

"Yes," Mr Monkey told her. "My brain always works **much** better when I eat jam."

Rosie went inside and came back with a slice of Swiss roll oozing with strawberry jam. "Will this be OK?"

"More than OK!" said Mr Monkey. He licked all the jam off and put the rest of the Swiss roll slice on his head. "Jam and a new hat!"

28

Rosie giggled. "It's quite a sticky hat, Mr Monkey. I'll make you a proper hat if you want."

"A hat of my own?" Mr Monkey turned a cartwheel and jumped into her arms.

"I like you, Rosie. And now I've eaten that jam, my brain is running as quickly as a chimp who's just seen a banana. I have an amazing, marvellous **monkey-tastic** plan! At tea-time tomorrow, we'll teach that cousin of yours to believe in fairies again. Just you wait and see!"

Chapter Four

Mr Monkey and Rosie had a
lovely afternoon. They played
with the fairy houses and Rosie
made Mr Monkey the hat she
had promised.

It was a bit big and fell down
over one eye but Mr Monkey was
delighted with it and refused to
take it off.

"Oh, Mr Monkey, it's so much fun having you here," Rosie whispered that night.

While she was asleep, Mr Monkey tiptoed over to the window. It was time for him to put his Monkey Masterplan into action!

Rosie found it difficult to concentrate in class the next day. Mr Monkey sat beside her on her desk. Whenever she looked at him, he winked.

At the end of school, he whispered, "Tell Katie that you want to play by the oak tree and get ready for a surprise!"

Rosie's tummy tingled with excitement.

"I suppose you want to play fairy games," Katie said, when they got back to Rosie's house. "Race you to the oak tree!"

Rosie stared after her. If she didn't know better she would have thought Katie actually wanted to play fairy games.

Mr Monkey jumped out of her bag. "Bouncing bananas! This is all going very well!" Sparks shot from his tail. "Come on, Rosie! Catch up with her and see the surprise!"

Rosie ran after Katie, her heart beating fast. What would be waiting outside?

Chapter Five

As Rosie reached the oak tree with Katie, she saw something that made her skid to a halt.

Fairies! There were fairies
flying round its trunk. She gasped.

Katie looked at her. "What's the
matter?" she asked.

"Fairies!" Rosie spluttered.

Katie frowned. "What are you talking about?"

"Can't you see them?" Rosie said.

Katie looked confused. "No. Is this a new game?"

One of the fairies tickled
Katie's nose.

Katie gave a squeal. "What
was that?"

More of the fairies joined in.
"Something's tickling me,"
she cried.

"It's fairies!" Rosie said. The swooping, fluttering creatures were beautiful – just like she had always imagined. "Oh, Katie, they're amazing!"

"But why can't I see them?"
Katie said in dismay.

Mr Monkey poked his head
up. "Because they won't show
themselves until you say you
believe in them, you silly banana!"

Katie opened and shut her mouth. "Mr Monkey's alive!"

"Alive and kicking!" Mr Monkey said. "I thought you didn't believe in magic, Katie?" He put his head on one side. "You know something? I think you do."

Katie looked ashamed. "You're right ... I do."

Rosie was surprised. "But at school you said fairies were babyish and you didn't believe in magic."

"I only said that because I didn't want to get teased," said Katie. "All my friends in Class Three say magic's for babies. I'm sorry. I've missed playing fairies with you. I really do believe in them."

"Oh, Katie!" Rosie said, hugging her in delight.

A pink haze shimmered
through the air and Katie gave
a cry of delight. "Oh, wow! I can
see them!"

The fairies giggled. "Hello,
Katie!"

A fairy landed on Rosie's hand. "It's lovely to finally meet you both. We often sleep in the fairy houses you made."

"We were really excited when Mr Monkey invited us to come to a tea party," said another fairy.

"But where is the tea party, Mr Monkey?" asked the first fairy.

"Silly me. I knew I'd forgotten something!" said Mr Monkey. He waved his tail. "Ta-da!" A shower of rainbow sparks shot into the air and a picnic appeared on the grass. Mr Monkey grinned. "Now the fun will **really** begin!"

Chapter Six

It was the best tea party ever.
There were sugarplums to eat,
along with wild strawberries,
wobbling jellies, a tower of iced
fairy cakes and an enormous pot
of strawberry jam.

"This is wonderful, Mr Monkey!" said Rosie.

"All we're missing is presents," said Mr Monkey. "Every tea party needs presents!"

He waved his tail again and
Rosie and Katie found themselves
holding two parcels wrapped in
sparkly paper. There were wings
inside!

"Put them on," said Mr Monkey.

The girls put their wings on and tied the ribbons. The wings began to flutter and all of a sudden Rosie and Katie were flying into the sky.

"This is amazing!" cried Rosie.

Mr Monkey cartwheeled
round the tree as the girls played
tag with the fairies.

"I'm always going to remember this day!" said Rosie.

"Me too," said Katie. Her cheeks were flushed and her eyes were shining.

Rosie felt a warm glow spread from her head to toes. Mr Monkey had given her an amazing time, but best of all she had her friend back – nothing could be better than that!

When the party was over, Mr Monkey magicked away the tea things, the girls' wings faded and the fairies flew off in a glittering crowd.

Katie told Rosie that even though she might pretend to her friends at school that she didn't believe in fairies, she wouldn't pretend with Rosie any more.

Rosie got ready for bed feeling very happy. She started writing Mr Monkey's diary.

"I wonder what Miss Preston will say when she reads this," she said to Mr Monkey. "I bet she won't believe it."

"You never know. Some grown-ups do believe in magic," said Mr Monkey.

Rosie gave him a hug. "I'll be like that. I'll never get too old for magic!" she said.

Mr Monkey's eyes twinkled. **"Monkey-tastic,"** he said with a smile.

Mr Monkey invited the fairies to a tea party. Katie and me had wings. We flew in the sky. But Mr Monkey didn't.

What an exciting adventure, Rosie. I'm sure Mr Monkey had fun.

He did!

What are you going to read next?

Have more adventures with
Horrid Henry,

or save the day with Anthony Ant!

Become a
superhero with Monstar,

float off to
sea with
Algy,

or have your very own Pirates' Picnic.

Grow carrots with

Lottie and Dottie,

make magic with
The Witch Dog,

and cast a spell with

The Three
Little Magicians.

Enjoy all the Early Readers.